IT'S A WOMAN'S WORLD

IT'S A WOMAN'S WORLD

A CENTURY OF WOMEN'S VOICES
IN POETRY

EDITED BY NEIL PHILIP

DUTTON CHILDREN'S BOOKS * NEW YORK

FOR SYLVIA WITH LOVE

Selection and Introduction copyright © 2000 by Neil Philip
Volume copyright © 2000 by The Albion Press Ltd
For copyright of individual poems and photographs, see the
Acknowledgments and Picture Credits on pages 91–93, which
constitute an extension of this copyright page.

CIP Data is available.

Published in the United States 2000 by Dutton Children's Books,
a division of Penguin Putnam Books for Young Readers
345 Hudson Street, New York, New York 10014

Conceived, designed, and produced by The Albion Press Ltd, England
Designed by Emma Bradford

Printed in Hong Kong/China by South China Printing Co. (1988) Ltd
First American Edition
ISBN 0-525-46328-3
10 9 8 7 6 5 4 3 2 1

CONTENTS

A Freedom Song

Domestic Economy

Power

I LIVE WITH A BULLET

THE OLD WOMEN GATHERED

INTRODUCTION

> This is my letter to the World
> That never wrote to Me—
> *Emily Dickinson*

Emily Dickinson, the finest woman poet of nineteenth-century America, lived a quiet, private life and never sought publication or fame. For her, it was enough to bring her poems to perfection in the echo chamber of her own mind. For although as a woman she was reserved and shy, as a poet she was daring and adventurous. Both editors and readers were frightened by the unfettered freedom of her verse. Early editions of her work try to harness that freedom by "correcting" her quirks, such as her unorthodox use of dashes to catch the rhythm of her thoughts.

It was not until the 1960s, with the work of such poets as Sylvia Plath and Anne Sexton, that women poets were free to lay bare their souls in public, as Emily Dickinson had done in private. In Dickinson's day, women poets were called poetesses, and they were expected to confine themselves to women's subjects and women's forms. Wistful lyrics about yearning and loss, or idyllic nature poems, were considered most suitable; the world of ideas and the world of action were reserved for men. Women poets who ventured into male territory—such as Elizabeth Barrett Browning in her 11,000-line verse novel *Aurora Leigh,* about the life of a woman writer and the role of women in society—were considered dangerous radicals.

The ideal was someone like the English poet Christina Rossetti, born in the same year as Dickinson, who wrote exquisite poems for children and somber adult lyrics about unhappy love and religious devotion. Her most popular poem, "Remember," ends with a plea that after her death she should be completely forgotten, even by her friends:

> Better by far you should forget and smile
> Than that you should remember and be sad.

This image of the self-effacing poetess with a retiring nature and a suffering soul was to be shattered by the social and cultural upheavals that shaped the twentieth century, a century in which women poets have raised Emily Dickinson's muted whisper to a triumphant shout.

The ways in which women poets have found the strength to raise their voices have been various. In the case of the Russian poet Anna Akhmatova, for instance, her strength was a response to the political repression that censored her into silence. Her "letter to the world" had to be as private, and as explosively potent, as Emily Dickinson's.

Akhmatova's long poem "Requiem" recalls her experience standing in line outside the prison in Leningrad after her son was arrested in one of Stalin's purges. She waited in line every day for seventeen months, along with others hoping for news of their loved ones. Her preface to the poem recalls how, one day, another woman in the queue recognized her:

> Now she started out of the torpor common to us all and asked me
> in a whisper (everyone whispered there):
> > "Can you describe this?"
> > And I said: "I can."
> > Then something like a smile passed fleetingly over what had once been
> her face.

Akhmatova's poem was composed between 1935 and 1940 on scraps of paper, which she learned by heart and then destroyed. She carried the poem's fourteen sections in her memory for more than twenty years; it was not safe to publish it until 1963, and then only abroad. In it, Akhmatova amplified the whisper from that prison queue into a howl of pain.

The power of poetry such as Anna Akhmatova's echoes through this book. I have selected work by women poets from all over the world to bear witness to women's lives in this most turbulent of centuries, in the course of which the women's movement has changed attitudes and expectations throughout the world. Nineteenth-century poems are full of warnings to girls not to venture out too far. Edna St. Vincent Millay—one of the poets who redefined women's themes in the early years of this century—remembered such cautions in a rueful little poem entitled "The Unexplorer":

> There was a road ran past our house
> Too lovely to explore.
> I asked my mother once—she said
> That if you followed where it led
> It brought you to the milk-man's door.
> (That's why I have not travelled more.)

Today, in her luminous poem "Power," a mother such as Alma Luz Villanueva gives very different advice to her daughter. "Take your power and fly," she writes, "like all/the women before you."

The new sense of freedom and control is beautifully summed up in the poem "Vierge Moderne" (which might be translated as "Modern Maiden") by the Finnish poet Edith Södergran:

I am a flame, searching and brave,
I am water, deep yet bold only to the knees,
I am fire and water, honestly combined, on free terms . . .

They are lines that could have been written by any number of the poets in this book—such as Anna Wickham, "free woman and poet," who wanted all her books to be prefaced by these lines:

Here is no sacrificial I,
Here are more I's than yet were in one human,
Here I reveal our common mystery:
I give you *woman*.

Anna Wickham's poem "The Marriage," included in the first section of this book, "Dear Female Heart," shows an attitude to love and marriage that would have been unthinkable in previous generations, which idealized the wife's role as that of "The Angel in the House," to quote the title of a long poem about married love by the Victorian poet Coventry Patmore. Anna Wickham's first line ("What a great battle you and I have fought!") shows a fighting spirit that would have shocked Coventry Patmore to the core, but which would have pleased the novelist Virginia Woolf, who in a 1931 lecture spoke of the need for women writers to "kill the Angel in the House."

The poets collected in this anthology all share this spirit of freedom and self-possession. In asserting that spirit, they do not reject the domestic preoccupations of previous generations, but revalue them. Navajo poet Luci Tapahonso's "All I Want" sees the art of making bread not as a household chore but as a craft and a mystery; the Australian poet Rosemary Dobson's "Folding the Sheets" does the same for a simple yet satisfying task that unites women the world over: "From Burma, from Lapland, / From India . . . / From China . . ."

The art of these poems is no less for serving such homely subjects. These are poets who are confidently able to write about whatever is on their minds and make it interesting and important—whether reducing complex issues to their simple essence or showing us the complex subtleties of simple things.

This book is arranged in seven sections that focus on different themes, such as childhood, growing up, falling in love, making a home, developing inner strength, using that strength to survive war and heartache, and growing old. The voices of the poets are as varied and individual as the women themselves, but they form a powerful and self-confident chorus. And the song they are singing? In the words of the Irish poet Eavan Boland, "It's a woman's world."

Neil Philip 15

IT'S A WOMAN'S WORLD

Our way of life
has hardly changed
since a wheel first
whetted a knife.

Maybe flame
burns more greedily,
and wheels are steadier
but we're the same

who milestone
our lives
with oversights—
living by the lights

of the loaf left
by the cash register,
the washing powder
paid for and wrapped,

the wash left wet:
like most historic peoples
we are defined
by what we forget,

by what we never will be—
star-gazers,
fire-eaters.
It's our alibi

for all time:
as far as history goes
we were never
on the scene of the crime.

So when the king's head
gored its basket—
grim harvest—
we were gristing bread

or getting the recipe
for a good soup
to appetize
our gossip.

It's still the same.
By night our windows
moth our children
to the flame

of hearth not history.
And still no page
scores the low music
of our outrage.

Appearances
still reassure:
that woman there,
craned to the starry mystery

is merely getting a breath
of evening air,
while this one here—
her mouth

a burning plume—
she's no fire-eater,
just my frosty neighbor
coming home.

EAVAN BOLAND

DEAR FEMALE HEART

DEAR FEMALE HEART

Dear Female Heart, I am sorry for you,
You must suffer, that is all that you can do.
But if you like, in common with the rest of the human race,
You may also look most absurd with a miserable face.

STEVIE SMITH

from RETURN TO FRANKFURT

The girl thinks   if I can only manage
not to step on any of these
delicate hands of shadow
cast on the sidewalk by the chestnut trees

The boy thinks   if I reach the trolley
in time and if it doesn't have to wait
at the switch and the traffic policeman really
does his job and tries to clear the street

If   thinks the girl   before I reach that tree
the third on the left no nun comes out at me
and if not more than twice I pass small boys
crossing the street in groups, carrying toys
oh   then it's certain that we'll meet

Unless   the boy thinks   there's a power failure
unless forked lightning strikes the driver
unless the trolley-car gets smashed to bits
surely we'll meet   yes I can count on it

And many times the girl must shiver
And the boy think   will this last forever
until under the chestnut trees they meet,
wordless and smiling, in some quiet street.

MARIE LUISE KASCHNITZ
translated from the German by Beatrice Cameron

TELL ME AGAIN

Am I your only love—in the whole world—now?
Am I really the only object of your love?
If passions rage in your mind,
If love springs eternal in your heart—
Is it all meant for me? Tell me again.

Tell me right now, am I the one who inspires
All your dark thoughts, all your sadness?
Share with me what you feel, what you think.
Come, my love, pour into my heart
Whatever gives you so much pain.
Tell me again.

NIGÂR HANIM
translated from the Turkish by Tâlat S. Halman

from A VALENTINE
TO SHERWOOD ANDERSON

What Do I See

A very little snail.
A medium sized turkey.
A small band of sheep.
A fair orange tree.
All nice wives are like that.
Listen to them from here.
Oh.
You did not have an answer.
Here.
Yes.

Why Do You Feel Differently

Why do you feel differently about a very little snail and a big one.

Why do you feel differently about a medium sized turkey and a very large one.

Why do you feel differently about a small band of sheep and several sheep that are riding.

Why do you feel differently about a fair orange tree and one that has blossoms as well.

Oh very well.

All nice wives are like that.

To Be.

No Please.

To Be

They can please

Not to be

Do they please.

Not to be

Do they not please

Yes please.

Do they please

No please.

Do they not please

No please.

Do they please.

Please.

If you please.

And if you please.

And if they please

And they please.

To be pleased.

Not to be pleased.

Not to be displeased.

To be pleased and to please.

GERTRUDE STEIN

THE MARRIAGE

What a great battle you and I have fought!
A fight of sticks and whips and swords,
A one-armed combat,
For each held the left hand pressed close to the heart,
To save the caskets from assault.

How tenderly we guarded them;
I would keep mine and still have yours,
And you held fast to yours and coveted mine.
Could we have dropt the caskets
We would have thrown down weapons
And been at each other like apes,
Scratching, biting, hugging
In exasperation.

What a fight!
Thank God that I was strong as you,
And you, though not my master, were my match.
How we panted; we grew dizzy with rage.
We forgot everything but the fight and the love of the caskets.

These we called by great names—
Personality, Liberty, Individuality.

Each fought for right to keep himself a slave
And to redeem his fellow.
How can this be done?

But the fight ended.
For both was victory
For both there was defeat.
Through blood we saw the caskets on the floor.
Our jewels were revealed;
An ugly toad in mine,
While yours was filled with most contemptible small snakes:
One held my vanity, the other held your sloth.

The fight is over, and our eyes are clear.—
Good friend, shake hands.

ANNA WICKHAM

AFTER EIGHT YEARS OF MARRIAGE

After eight years of marriage
The first time I visited my parents,
They asked, "Are you happy, tell us."
It was an absurd question
And I should have laughed at it.
Instead, I cried,
And in between sobs, nodded yes.
I wanted to tell them
That I was happy on Tuesday.
I was unhappy on Wednesday.
I was happy one day at 8 o'clock
I was most unhappy by 8.15.
I wanted to tell them how one day
We all ate a watermelon and laughed.
I wanted to tell them how I wept in bed all night once
And struggled hard from hurting myself.
That it wasn't easy to be happy in a family of twelve.
But they were looking at my two sons,
Hopping around like young goats.
Their wrinkled hands, beaten faces and grey eyelashes
Were all too much too real.
So I swallowed everything,
And smiled a smile of great content.

MAMTA KALIA

SUNG IN A GRAVEYARD

O I'm a professional wife,
Tra la la
And I'm bound to the trade for my life,
Tra la la.
I hate to be slack
And I hope I'm not wrong,
But I find business hours most unbearably long,
As a thorough professional wife,
Tra la la.

I think in these organised days
They might run my poor job in relays;
I can work very well in the light,
But I'm tired of the business at night,
Although a professional wife,
Tra la la.

I'd carry a card-case and own a man's name,
I'd manage a house and take wage for the same;
But to bear a man's children, and share a man's bed,
Should never be paid for in boots and in bread,
If a wench has the heart of a wife.
Tra la la.

ANNA WICKHAM

WOMAN

She, the river,
said to him, the sea:
     All my life
     I've been dissolving myself
     and flowing towards you
     for your sake
     in the end it was I
     who turned into the sea
     a woman's gift
     is as large as the sky
          but you went on
          worshipping yourself
          you never thought
          of becoming a river
          and merging
          with me

HIRA BANSODE
translated from the Marathi by Vinay Dharwadker

CHANT FOR DARK HOURS

Some men, some men
Cannot pass a
Book shop.
(Lady, make your mind up, and wait your life away.)

Some men, some men
Cannot pass a
Crap game.
(He said he'd come at moonrise, and here's another day!)

Some men, some men
Cannot pass a
Bar-room.
(Wait about, and hang about, and that's the way it goes.)

Some men, some men
Cannot pass a
Woman.
(Heaven never send me another one of those!)

Some men, some men
Cannot pass a
Golf course.
(Read a book, and sew a seam, and slumber if you can.)

Some men, some men
Cannot pass a
Haberdasher's.
(All your life you wait around for some damn man!)

NEWS OF A BABY

News of a Baby

Welcome, baby, to the world of swords
And deadlier words.
We offer you a rough bed, and tears at morning,
And soon a playground
Bounded by ice and stones,
A buttonhole of thorns,
A kiss on war's corner.

We promise you, baby,
The stumble of fear in the heart,
The lurch of fear in the bones.

Painted upon your mother's cheek already
I see the dark effusion of your blood,
Bending already beside her patient chair the bandaged ghosts.

Welcome, baby, no dread thing will be omitted.
We are your eager hosts.

ELIZABETH RIDDELL

My Baby Has No Name Yet

My baby has no name yet;
like a new-born chick or a puppy,
my baby is not named yet.

What numberless texts I examined
at dawn and night and evening over again!
But not one character did I find
which is as lovely as the child.

Starry field of the sky,
or heap of pearls in the depth.
Where can the name be found, how can I?

My baby has no name yet;
like an unnamed bluebird or white flowers
from the farthest land for the first,
I have no name for this baby of ours.

KIM NAM-JO
translated from the Korean by Ko Won

Morning Song

Love set you going like a fat gold watch.
The midwife slapped your footsoles, and your bald cry
Took its place among the elements.

Our voices echo, magnifying your arrival. New statue.
In a drafty museum, your nakedness
Shadows our safety. We stand round blankly as walls.

I'm no more your mother
Than the cloud that distils a mirror to reflect its own slow
Effacement at the wind's hand.

All night your moth-breath
Flickers among the flat pink roses. I wake to listen:
A far sea moves in my ear.

One cry, and I stumble from bed, cow-heavy and floral
In my Victorian nightgown.
Your mouth opens clean as a cat's. The window square

Whitens and swallows its dull stars. And now you try
Your handful of notes;
The clear vowels rise like balloons.

SYLVIA PLATH

ESKIMO OCCASION

I am in my Eskimo-hunting-song mood,
Aha!
The lawn is tundra   the car will not start
the sunlight is an avalanche   we are avalanche-struck at our
   breakfast
struck with sunlight through glass   me and my spoonfed daughters
out of this world in our kitchen.

I will sing the song of my daughter-hunting,
Oho!
The waves lay down   the ice grew strong
I sang the song   of dark water under ice
the song of winter fishing   the magic for seal rising
among the ancestor-masks.

I waited by water to dream new spirits,
Hoo!
The water spoke   the ice shouted
the sea opened   the sun made young shadows
they breathed my breathing   I took them from deep water
I brought them fur-warmed home.

I am dancing the years of the two great hunts,
Ya-hay!
It was I who waited   cold in the wind-break
I stamp like the bear   I call like the wind of the thaw
I leap like the sea spring-running.   My sunstruck daughters
   splutter
and chuckle and bang their spoons:

Mummy is singing at breakfast and dancing!
So big!

JUDITH RODRIGUEZ

30

MOMMA SAYINGS

Momma had words for us:
We were "crumb crushers,"
"eating machines,"
"bottomless pits."
Still, she made us charter members
of the bonepickers' club,
saying, "Just don't let your eyes
get bigger than your stomach."
Saying, "Take all you want,
but eat all you take."
Saying, "I'm not made of money, you know,
and the man at the Safeway
don't give away groceries for free."

She trained us not to leave lights on
"all over the house,"
because "electricity costs money
so please turn the lights off when you leave a room
and take the white man's hand out of my pocket."

When we were small
she called our feet "ant mashers,"
but each time we'd outgrow our shoes,
our feet became "platforms."
She told us we must be growing big feet
to support some big heavyset women
(like our grandma Tiddly).

When she had to buy us new underwear
to replace the old ones full of holes,
she'd swear we were growing razor blades in our behinds,
"you tear these draws up so fast."

Momma had words for us, all right:
she called us "the wrecking crew."
She said our untidy bedroom
looked like "a cyclone struck it."

Our dirty fingernails she called "victory gardens."
And when we'd come in from playing outside
she'd tell us, "You girls smell like iron rust."
She'd say, "Go take a bath
and get some of that funk off of you."
But when the water ran too long in the tub
she'd yell, "That's enough water to wash an elephant."
And after the bath she'd say,
"Be sure and grease those ashy legs."
She'd lemon-creme our elbows
and pull the hot comb
through "these tough kinks on your heads."

Momma had lots of words for us,
her never-quite-perfect daughters,
the two brown pennies
she wanted to polish
so we'd shine like dimes.

HARRYETTE MULLEN

They Were Alone in the Winter

Each night, I braid my daughter's hair.
My fingers slip through the thick silkiness,
weaving the strands into a single black stream.

"The air feels like something will happen,"
she says. "Maybe it will snow."
The moon outside is a silver arc in the cold sky.
"In the old stories, they say the moon comes as a beautiful horse,"
I tell her. From the bedroom window, we look out
                              at the glistening night sky.

It is outside the house: the frozen night.
It glimmers with her pleas for snow.
It glimmers in her night dreams: a fusing of music, laughter,
                              talk of boys and clothes.
It glimmers here in the fibers of my bed sheets,
            there above the old roar of the Kaw River.
It glimmers in the western sky where he thinks of me and smiles.

In an old story, a woman and her daughter were alone in the winter
and the mother said, "Tomorrow, if the sun rises,
                        it will come as many different horses."

LUCI TAPAHONSO

POEM FOR MY SISTER

My little sister likes to try my shoes,
to strut in them,
admire her spindle-thin twelve-year-old legs
in this season's styles.
She says they fit her perfectly,
but wobbles
on their high heels, they're
hard to balance.

I like to watch my little sister
playing hopscotch, admire the neat hops-and-skips of her,
their quick peck,
never-missing their mark, not
over-stepping the line.
She is competent at peever.

I try to warn my little sister
about unsuitable shoes,
point out my own distorted feet, the callouses,
odd patches of hard skin.
I should not like to see her
in my shoes.
I wish she could stay
sure footed,
   sensibly shod.

LIZ LOCHHEAD

TWIRLING

Spring and the girls are twirling batons,
learning *beginnings* and *endings*,
aerials, swings, salutes, capers, wraps.
Everywhere batons spin and bounce.
The girls' wrists ache. They have chapped
hands, sore calves and thighs.
Twirling drives them to bed early.

Beth Skudder and Mary Lou Ravese,
captains of the varsity twirling team,
send messages: "Use imagination!
It's always nice to see something new."

They will progress with time from *butterflies*
to *tea cup slides* and *rainbow reverses*,
set their wands on fire,
become the hubs of chancy wheels.

In Beth Skudder's dream, she does the
heliocopter on the gym roof,
creating a field of force no one can enter.
Soon she begins to rise, still twirling,
over the track, the trees, the parking lot.

She's a space probe, asking what's out there,
waving good-bye to the twirlers below,
whose bodies shimmer, then dim, like lights
from a little town quickly passed over.

JANE FLANDERS

THE GOOD TEACHERS

You run round the back to be in it again.
No bigger than your thumbs, those virtuous women
size you up from the front row. Soon now,
Miss Ross will take you for double History.
You breathe on the glass, making a ghost of her, say
South Sea Bubble Defenestration of Prague.

You love Miss Pirie. So much, you are top
of her class. So much, you need two of you
to stare out from the year, serious, passionate.
The River's Tale by Rudyard Kipling by heart.
Her kind intelligent green eye. Her cruel blue one.
You are making a poem up for her in your head.

But not Miss Sheridan. Comment vous appelez.
But not Miss Appleby. Equal to the square
of the other two sides. Never Miss Webb.
Dar es Salaam. Kilimanjaro. Look. The good teachers
swish down the corridor in long, brown skirts,
snobbish and proud and clean and qualified.

And they've got your number. You roll the waistband
of your skirt over and over, all leg, all
dumb insolence, smoke-rings. You won't pass.
You could do better. But there's the wall you climb
into dancing, lovebites, marriage, the Cheltenham
and Gloucester, today. The day you'll be sorry one day.

A FREEDOM SONG

A Freedom Song

Atieno washes dishes,
Atieno plucks the chicken,
Atieno gets up early,
Beds her sacks down in the kitchen,
Atieno eight years old,
Atieno yo.

Since she is my sister's child
Atieno needs no pay,
While she works my wife can sit
Sewing every sunny day:
With her earnings I support
Atieno yo.

Atieno's sly and jealous,
Bad example to the kids
Since she minds them, like a schoolgirl
Wants their dresses, shoes and beads,
Atieno ten years old,
Atieno yo.

Now my wife has gone to study
Atieno is less free.
Don't I keep her, school my own ones,
Pay the party, union fee,
All for progress: aren't you grateful
Atieno yo?

Visitors need much attention,
All the more when I work night.
That girl spends too long at market,
Who will teach her what is right?
Atieno is rising fourteen,
Atieno yo.

Atieno's had a baby
So we know that she is bad.
Fifty fifty it may live
And repeat the life she had
Ending in post-partum bleeding,
Atieno yo.

Atieno's soon replaced.
Meat and sugar more than all
She ate in such a narrow life
Were lavished on her funeral.
Atieno's gone to glory,
Atieno yo.

MARJORIE OLUDHE MACGOYE

SONG FOR A YOUNG GIRL'S PUBERTY CEREMONY

I am on my way running,
I am on my way running,
Looking toward me is the edge of the world,
I am trying to reach it,
The edge of the world does not look far away,
To that I am on my way running.

TRADITIONAL, PAPAGO
translated from the Papago by Frances Densmore

To a Daughter Leaving Home

When I taught you
at eight to ride
a bicycle, loping along
beside you
as you wobbled away
on two round wheels,
my own mouth rounding
in surprise when you pulled
ahead down the curved
path of the park,
I kept waiting
for the thud
of your crash as I
sprinted to catch up,
while you grew
smaller, more breakable
with distance,
pumping, pumping
for your life, screaming
with laughter,
the hair flapping
behind you like a
handkerchief waving
goodbye.

LINDA PASTAN

SISTERS

(for Marian)

My sister
was the bad one—
said what she thought
and did what she liked
and didn't care.

At ten she wore
a knife tucked in
her leather belt,
dreamed of *being*
a prince on a white horse.

Became a dolly bird
with dyed hair longer
than her skirts, pulling
the best of the local talent.
Mother wept and prayed.

At thirty she's divorced,
has cropped her locks
and squats in Hackney—
tells me "God created man
then realised Her mistake."

I'm not like her,
I'm good—but now
I'm working on it.
Fighting through
to my own brand of badness.

I am glad of her
at last—her conferences,
her anger, and her boots.
We talk and smoke
and laugh at everybody—

two bad sisters.

WENDY COPE

MY SISTER, THE EMPRESS

My sister, the empress
became cross with us
she took her crowns and went away
but mother and father believe
that she'll come back some day.

She is sure to come back, says father
why, how could anyone
from one kingdom to another go
with only her slippers on.

But mother has a woman's heart
she says it wouldn't be right
for her daughter to wear a crown and slippers
out in broad daylight.

She'll come tonight, says mother
she'll come tomorrow, says father
I alone know that my sister is gone
forever.

I have seen the place where she has passed
strewn with the seven crowns
so her parents wouldn't be aware
and I tracked down her slippers
in that other kingdom there.

ILEANA MĂLĂNCIOIU
translated from the Romanian by Dan Duțescu

MY WICKED WICKED WAYS

This is my father.
See? He is young.
He looks like Errol Flynn.
He is wearing a hat
that tips over one eye,
a suit that fits him good,
and baggy pants.
He is also wearing
those awful shoes,
the two-toned ones
my mother hates.

Here is my mother.
She is not crying.
She cannot look into the lens
because the sun is bright.
The woman,
the one my father knows,
is not here.
She does not come till later.

My mother will get very mad.
Her face will turn red
and she will throw one shoe.
My father will say nothing.
After a while everyone
will forget it.
Years and years will pass.
My mother will stop mentioning it.

This is me she is carrying.
I am a baby.
She does not know
I will turn out bad.

SANDRA CISNEROS

Yet Still

I have been encouraged to wait
                   outside the door
to wait in an empty room
                   to wait for a
turn of a knob
                   to wait
for a room to fill
                   to wait and
be patient.
                   I have been encouraged.
I have waited outside the door
                   without word or hope
outside with space for company
                   outside
I have waited.
Inside you have sat
                   sitting inside
behind a door
                   sitting inside
a big room
                   sitting inside
safe from me
                   outside
where I have waited
                   tired of waiting
your door opens slowly
                   I am waiting.

DOMESTIC ECONOMY

DOMESTIC ECONOMY

I will have few cooking-pots,
They shall be bright,
They shall reflect to blinding
God's straight light.
I will have four garments,
They shall be clean,
My service shall be good,
Though my diet be mean.
Then I shall have excess to give the poor,
And right to counsel beggars at my door.

ANNA WICKHAM

MY MAMA MOVED AMONG THE DAYS

My Mama moved among the days
like a dreamwalker in a field;
seemed like what she touched was hers
seemed like what touched her couldn't hold,
she got us almost through the high grass
then seemed like she turned around and ran
right back in
right back on in

LUCILLE CLIFTON

ALL I WANT

All I want is the bread to turn out like hers just once
              brown crust
              soft, airy insides
              rich and round
that is all.
So I ask her: How many cups?
              Ah yaa ah, she says,
              tossing flour and salt into a large silver bowl.
              I don't measure with cups.
              I just know by my hands,
              just a little like this is right, see?
              You young people always ask
              those kinds of questions,
              she says,
thrusting her arms into the dough
and turning it over and over again.
The table trembles with her movements.
I watch silently and this coffee is good,
                          strong and fresh.
              Outside, her son is chopping wood,
              his body an intense arc.
              The dull rhythm of winter
              is the swinging of the axe
              and the noise of children squeezing in
              with the small sighs of wind
              through the edges of the windows.

She pats and tosses it furiously
shaping balls of warm, soft dough.
              There, we'll let it rise,
              she says, sitting down now.
              We drink coffee and there is nothing
              like the warm smell of bread rising
              on windy, woodchopping afternoons.

LUCI TAPAHONSO

MRS. SMALL

Mrs. Small went to the kitchen for her pocketbook
And came back to the living room with a peculiar look
And the coffee pot.
Pocketbook. Pot.
Pot. Pocketbook.

The insurance man was waiting there
With superb and cared-for hair.
His face did not have much time.
He did not glance with sublime
Love upon the little plump tan woman
With the half-open mouth and the half-mad eyes
And the smile half-human
Who stood in the middle of the living-room floor planning
        apple pies
And graciously offering him a steaming coffee pot.
Pocketbook. Pot.

"Oh!" Mrs. Small came to her senses,
Peered earnestly through thick lenses,
Jumped terribly. This, too, was a mistake,
Unforgivable no matter how much she had to bake.
For there can be no whiter whiteness than this one:
An insurance man's shirt on its morning run.
This Mrs. Small now soiled
With a pair of brown
Spurts (just recently boiled)
Of the "very best coffee in town."

"The best coffee in town is what *you* make, Delphine! There
        is none dandier!"
Those were the words of the pleased Jim Small—
Who was no bandier of words at all.
Jim Small was likely to give you a good swat
When he was *not*
Pleased. He was, absolutely, no bandier.

"I don't know where my mind is this morning,"
Said Mrs. Small, scorning
Apologies! For there was so much
For which to apologize! Oh such
Mountains of things, she'd never get anything done
If she begged forgiveness for each one.

She paid him.

But apologies and her hurry would not mix.
The six
Daughters were a-yell, a-scramble, in the hall. The four
Sons (horrors) could not be heard any more.

No.
The insurance man would have to glare
Idiotically into her own sterile stare
A moment—then depart,
Leaving her to release her heart
And dizziness

And silence her six
And mix
Her spices and core
And slice her apples, and find her four.
Continuing her part
Of the world's business.

GWENDOLYN BROOKS

PORTRAIT BY A NEIGHBOR

Before she has her floor swept
   Or her dishes done,
Any day you'll find her
   A-sunning in the sun!

It's long after midnight
   Her key's in the lock,
And you never see her chimney smoke
   Till past ten o'clock!

She digs in her garden
   With a shovel and a spoon,
She weeds her lazy lettuce
   By the light of the moon,

She walks up the walk
   Like a woman in a dream,
She forgets she borrowed butter
   And pays you back cream!

Her lawn looks like a meadow,
   And if she mows the place
She leaves the clover standing
   And the Queen Anne's lace!

EDNA ST. VINCENT MILLAY

FOLDING THE SHEETS

You and I will fold the sheets
Advancing towards each other
From Burma, from Lapland,

From India where the sheets have been washed in the river
And pounded upon stones:
Together we will match the corners.

From China where women on either side of the river
Have washed their pale cloth in the White Stone Shallows
"Under the shining moon."

We meet as though in the formal steps of a dance
To fold the sheets together, put them to air
In wind, in sun over bushes, or by the fire.

We stretch and pull from one side and then the other—
Your turn. Now mine.
We fold them and put them away until they are needed.

A wish for all people when they lie down in bed—
Smooth linen, cool cotton, the fragrance and stir of herbs
And the faint but perceptible scent of sweet clear water.

ROSEMARY DOBSON

"I TAUGHT MYSELF TO LIVE SIMPLY AND WISELY"

I taught myself to live simply and wisely,
to look at the sky and pray to God,
and to wander long before evening
to tire my useless sadness.

When the burdocks rustle in the ravine
and the yellow-red rowanberry cluster droops

I write down happy verses
about life's decay, decay and beauty.

I come back. The fluffy cat
licks my palm, purrs so sweetly,
and the fire flares bright
on the saw-mill turret by the lake.

Only the cry of a stork landing on the roof
occasionally breaks the silence.
If you knock on my door
I may not even hear.

ANNA AKHMATOVA
translated from the Russian by Richard McKane

PROPHECY

I shall lie hidden in a hut
   In the middle of an alder wood,
With the back door blind and bolted shut,
   And the front door locked for good.

I shall lie folded like a saint,
   Lapped in a scented linen sheet,
On a bedstead striped with bright-blue paint,
   Narrow and cold and neat.

The midnight will be glassy black
   Behind the panes, with wind about
To set his mouth against a crack
   And blow the candle out.

ELINOR WYLIE

ELEGY FOR A WOMAN
OF NO IMPORTANCE

When she died no face turned pale, no lips trembled
doors heard no retelling of her death
no curtains opened to air the room of grief
no eyes followed the coffin to the end of the road—
only, hovering in the memory, a vague form
                passing in the lane

The scrap of news stumbled in the alleyways
its whisper, finding no shelter,
lodged obscurely in an unseen corner.
The moon murmured sadly.

Night, unconcerned, gave way to morning
light came with the milk cart and the call to fasting
with the hungry mewing of a cat of rags and bones
the shrill cries of vendors in the bitter streets
the squabbling of small boys throwing stones
dirty water spilling along the gutters
smells on the wind
which played about the rooftops
playing in deep forgetfulness
playing alone

NĀZIK AL-MALĀ'IKAH
translated from the Arabic by Chris Knipp and Mohammed Sadiq

POWER

POWER

You come from a line of
healing women: *doctoras*, *brujas*.

Doctors, sorceress. Though, actually,
in the Spanish dictionary, *brujo* is

sorcerer, conjurer, wizard—while
bruja is witch, hag, owl. Ha!

Then owl it shall be. Your great-
grandmother was an owl; your great-

great-grandmother was an owl,
and your mother is a witch,

a hag, and an owl. Witch and hag
has always—in time, only 5,000 years

before that Her magic and
Her beauty shone—meant a woman with

power; your great-great-grand
mother, Isidra, traveled Sonora

healing, and she married five
times, each time a better man;

your great-grandmother, Jesus, married
to a man of God, healed from wild

weeds and flowers picked from
vacant lots in Los Angeles.

Your grandmother, Lydia, heard
the healing music through her finger-

tips, but the music burned her:
witch, hag, witch. And I, your

mother, hear the word, healing
me, you, us, and though I burn,

I fly, too: owl, hawk, raven, my
eagle. Hummingbird, sparrow, jay,

mockingbird, snow owl, barn owl,
great-horned owl, pelican, golden

eagle. So, daughter, healer, take my
name: be a witch, a hag, a sorceress.

Take your power and fly like all
the women before you.

Fly Antoinetta Theresa
Villanueva.

ALMA LUZ VILLANUEVA

EARTH MOTHER

(*low singing is heard*)

old /   Bells. bells. bells.
woman's let the bells ring.
voice /   BELLS. BELLS. BELLS.
           ring the bells to announce
           this your earth mother.
           for the day is turning
           in my thighs And you are born
           BLACK GIRL.

           come, i am calling to you.
           this old earth mother of the elaborate dreams
           come. come nearer. girl. NEARER.
           i can almost see your face now.
           COME CLOSER.

Low /   yes. there you are. i have stuffed
laugh /   your whole history in my mouth
           i. your earth mother
           was that hungry once. for knowledge.
           come closer. ah little Black girl
           i see you.
           i can see you coming
           towards me little girl
           running from seven to thirty-five

           in one day.
           i can see you coming
           girl made of black braids
           i can see you coming
           in the arena of youth
           girl shaking your butt to double dutch days
           i can see you coming
           girl racing dawns
           i can see you coming
           girl made of black rain
           i can see you coming.

SONIA SANCHEZ

"Woman, you are afraid of the forest"

Woman, you are afraid of the forest
I see it in your eyes
when you stare into the darkness:
the terrified look of a defenceless creature.

Woman, *you* are a forest
strange and deep: I see
you are afraid of yourself.

MARIA WINE
translated from the Swedish by Nadia Christensen

UPPER BROADWAY

The leafbud straggles forth
toward the frigid light of the airshaft   this is faith
this pale extension of a day
when looking up   you know   something is changing
winter has turned   though the wind is colder
Three streets away   a roof collapses   onto people
who thought they still had time   Time out of mind

I have written so many words
wanting to live inside you
to be of use to you

Now I must write for myself   for this blind
woman scratching the pavement   with her wand of thought
this slippered crone   inching on icy streets
reaching into wire trashbaskets   pulling out
what was thrown away   and infinitely precious

I look at my hands and see   they are still unfinished
I look at the vine and see the leafbud
inching towards life

I look at my face in the glass   and see
a halfborn woman

ADRIENNE RICH

EVE

Beside the highway
at the motel door
      it roots
the last survivor of a pioneer
      orchard
miraculously   still
      bearing.

A thud   another apple falls
      I stoop   and O
that scent, gnarled, ciderish
      with sun in it
that woody pulp
      for teeth and tongue
      to bite and curl around
that spurting juice
      earth-sweet!

In fifty seconds, fifty summers sweep
      and shake me—
I am alive!   can stand
      up still
hoarding this apple
      in my hand.

DOROTHY LIVESAY

THE TRUTH IS

In my left pocket a Chickasaw hand
rests on the bone of the pelvis.
In my right pocket
a white hand. Don't worry. It's mine
and not some thief's.
It belongs to a woman who sleeps in a twin bed
even though she falls in love too easily,
and walks along with hands
in her own empty pockets
even though she has put them in others
for love not money.

About the hands, I'd like to say
I am a tree, grafted branches
bearing two kinds of fruit,
apricots maybe and pit cherries.
It's not that way. The truth is
we are crowded together
and knock against each other at night.
We want amnesty.

Linda, girl, I keep telling you
this is nonsense
about who loved who
and who killed who.

Here I am, taped together
like some old civilian conservation corps
passed by from the great depression
and my pockets are empty.
It's just as well since they are masks
for the soul, and since coins and keys
both have the sharp teeth of property.

Girl, I say,
it is dangerous to be a woman of two countries.
You've got your hands in the dark
of two empty pockets. Even though
you walk and whistle like you aren't afraid
you know which pocket the enemy lives in

and you remember how to fight
so you better keep right on walking.
And you remember who killed who.
For this you want amnesty
and there's that knocking on the door
in the middle of the night.

Relax, there are other things to think about.
Shoes for instance.
Now those are the true masks of the soul.
The left shoe
and the right one with its white foot.

LINDA HOGAN

Vierge Moderne

I am no woman, I am a neuter.
I am a child, a page-boy, and a bold decision,
I am a laughing streak of a scarlet sun . . .
I am a net for all voracious fish,
I am a toast to every woman's honor,
I am a step toward luck and toward ruin,
I am a leap in freedom and the self . . .
I am the whisper of desire in a man's ear,
I am the soul's shivering, the flesh's longing and denial,
I am an entry sign to new paradises.
I am a flame, searching and brave,
I am water, deep yet bold only to the knees,
I am fire and water, honestly combined, on free terms . . .

EDITH SÖDERGRAN
translated from the Swedish by Stina Katchadourian

To the Tune "The River Is Red"

How many wise men and heroes
Have survived the dust and dirt of the world?
How many beautiful women have been heroines?
There were the novel and famous women generals
Ch'in Liang-yü and Shen Yün-yin.
Though tears stained their dresses
Their hearts were full of blood.
The wild strokes of their swords
Whistled like dragons and sobbed with pain.

The perfume of freedom burns my mind
With grief for my country.
When will we ever be cleansed?
Comrades, I say to you,
Spare no effort, struggle unceasingly,
That at last peace may come to our people.
And jewelled dresses and deformed feet
Will be abandoned.
And one day, all under heaven
Will see beautiful free women,
Blooming like fields of flowers,
And bearing brilliant and noble human beings.

CH'IU CHIN
translated from the Chinese by Kenneth Rexroth and Ling Chung

HOLDING MY BEADS

Unforgiving as the course of justice
Inerasable as my scars and fate
I am here
a woman . . . . . with all my lives
strung out like beads
                              before me
It isn't privilege or pity
that I seek
It isn't reverence or safety
quick happiness or purity
                              but
the power to be what I am/a woman
charting my own futures/   a woman
holding my beads in my hand

GRACE NICHOLS

SURF

A mountain of books half-finished,
A mountain of manuscript papers half-written,
The massive wave of this winter night
Broke over me.
I'm surfing now.

NAGASE KIYOKO
translated from the Japanese by Kijima Hajime

I LIVE WITH A BULLET

I Live with a Bullet . . .

I live
with a bullet in my heart.
I'm not going to die so soon.
It is snowing.
Bright.
Children are playing.
One may weep,
one may sing.

Only I shall not sing and weep.
We live in town, not in the forest.

I shall forget nothing as it is,
all that I know, I shall carry in my heart.

The snowy, transparent, bright
Kazan winter asks:
"How will you live?"
I myself do not know.
"Will you survive?"
I do not know myself.

"How is it you did not die from the bullet?"

Already not far from the end,
I continued living,
not because
in a distant little Kamsk town,
where the midnights are bright with snow,
where hard frost makes itself felt,
my joy and immortality
picked themselves up and spoke.

"How is it you did not die from the bullet,
how did you survive the burning lead?"

I continued living,
not because, when I saw the end,
my heart, beating high,
managed to persuade me

I would be able one day
to tell of our suffering.

"How is it you did not die from the bullet,
how is it the blow did not lay you low?"

I continued living,
not because,
when no strength at all was left,
I saw
the day of victory
stirring,
dawning
over the remote railway stops,
the sidings choked with snow,
beyond the moving
tank masses,
the forests
of shouldered bayonets—
the earth lay in the shadow of its wing.

Through my own
and through the misfortunes of others
I walked, regardless of obstacles, toward that day.

MARGARITA ALIGER
translated from the Russian by Daniel Weissbort

The Second World War

The voice said "We are at War"
And I was afraid, for I did not know what this meant.
My sister and I ran to our friends next door
As if they could help. History was lessons learnt
      With ancient dates, but here

      Was something utterly new,
The radio, called the wireless then, had said
That the country would have to be brave. There was much to do.
And I remember that night as I lay in bed
      I thought of soldiers who

      Had stood on our nursery floor
Holding guns, on guard and stiff. But war meant blood
Shed over battle-fields, Cavalry galloping. War
On that September Sunday made us feel frightened
      Of what our world waited for.

ELIZABETH JENNINGS

CAN'T TELL

When World War II was declared
on the morning radio,
we glued our ears, widened our eyes.
Our bodies shivered.

A voice said
Japan was the enemy,
Pearl Harbor a shambles
and in our grocery store
in Berkeley, we were suspended

next to the meat market
where voices hummed,
valises, pots and pans packed,
no more hot dogs, baloney,
pork kidneys.

We children huddled on wooden planks
and my parents whispered:
We are Chinese, we are Chinese.
Safety pins anchored,
our loins ached.

Shortly our Japanese neighbors vanished
and my parents continued to whisper:
We are Chinese, we are Chinese.

We wore black arm bands,
put up a sign
in bold letters.

NELLIE WONG

LET US BE MIDWIVES!

An untold story of the atomic bombing

Night in the basement of a concrete structure now in ruins.
Victims of the atomic bomb
jammed the room;
it was dark—not even a single candle.
The smell of fresh blood, the stench of death,
    the closeness of sweaty people, the moans.
From out of all that, lo and behold, a voice:
"The baby's coming!"

In that hellish basement, at that very moment,
a young woman had gone into labor.
In the dark, without a single match, what to do?
People forgot their own pains, worried about her.
And then: "I'm a midwife. I'll help with the birth."
The speaker, seriously injured herself,
    had been moaning only moments before.
And so new life was born in the dark of that pit of hell.
And so the midwife died before dawn, still bathed in blood.
Let us be midwives!
Let us be midwives!
Even if we lay down our own lives to do so.

KURIHARA SADAKO
translated from the Japanese by Richard H. Minear

FREEDOM FIGHTER

A freedom fighter, she said
lighting the gas stove.
In the mountains we fought . . .
great days . . .
the words stubborn
weary in the shabby kitchen
with the yellowed fridge
and the tinted photograph
of the dead husband.
The house full of morose
rooms suffocated with rugs.

We came out on the low verandah
her heavy stockings pitch black
the rough spun dress the
indigo blue of some wild flower
the Sunday neighbourhood still asleep.
Come again, she said indifferently,
watching the windy street
and the Town Hall squatting
on its elephant legs,
come again.

ANTIGONE KEFALA

FEAR

Today the ghetto knows a different fear,
Close in its grip, Death wields an icy scythe.
An evil sickness spreads a terror in its wake,
The victims of its shadow weep and writhe.

Today a father's heartbeat tells his fright
And mothers bend their heads into their hands.
Now children choke and die with typhus here,
A bitter tax is taken from their bands.

My heart still beats inside my breast
While friends depart for other worlds.
Perhaps it's better—who can say?—
Than watching this, to die today?

No, no, my God, we want to live!
Not watch our numbers melt away.
We want to have a better world,
We want to work—we must not die!

EVA PICKOVÁ, 12 years old, Terezín Concentration Camp
translated from the Czech by Jeanne Němcová

To My Children

Others may pity me but you shall not be ashamed
how can I scorn the life which is all I have
I will not belittle the little that I have saved
by denying my childhood memories my love

How can I wish to undo the past which I am
though I beggared myself I would not become another
"the appalling Jewish experience" is my own
"the unknown victims" are my father and mother

Be proud of the beginning you have in me
be proud of how far I have wandered with this burden
I would value you less if I were not a refugee
your presence changes my wilderness to a garden

KAREN GERSHON

WHEN I WAS AT MY MOST BEAUTIFUL

When I was at my most beautiful
town after town came crashing down.
I caught glimpses of the blue sky
from the most unexpected places.

When I was at my most beautiful
people were dying all around me
in factories, at sea, on islands without names
I lost my chance to make the best of myself.

When I was at my most beautiful
none of the young men brought me tender gifts
all they knew how to do was salute
and set out for war, leaving only their glances behind.

When I was at my most beautiful
my head was empty
my mind obstinate
but my arms and legs shone like chestnuts.

When I was at my most beautiful
my country lost the war
how could all that have happened?
I rolled up my sleeves and marched around my humiliated town.

When I was at my most beautiful
jazz flowed from the radio
I devoured the sweet exotic sounds
the way I smoked my first forbidden cigarettes.

When I was at my most beautiful
I was so very unhappy
I was so very awkward
and so terribly lonely.

So I decided I'd live a very long time
Like old man Rouault
who painted his most beautiful works in his old age
if I could.

IBARAGI NORIKO
translated from the Japanese by Aoyami Miyuki and Leza Lowitz

THE OLD WOMEN GATHERED

. . . And the Old Women Gathered

The Gospel Singers

and the old women gathered
and sang His praises
standing
resolutely together
like supply sergeants who
have seen
everything
and are still
Regular Army: It
was fierce and
not melodic and
although we ran
the sound of it
stayed in our ears . . .

MARI EVANS

LINEAGE

My grandmothers were strong.
They followed plows and bent to toil.
They moved through fields sowing seed.

They touched earth and grain grew.
They were full of sturdiness and singing.
My grandmothers were strong.

My grandmothers are full of memories.
Smelling of soap and onions and wet clay
With veins rolling roughly over quick hands
They have many clean words to say.
My grandmothers were strong.
Why am I not as they?

MARGARET WALKER

ON A WINTER NIGHT

On a winter night
I sat alone
In a cold room,
Feeling old, strange
At the year's change,
In fire light.

Last fire of youth,
All brilliance burning,
And my year turning—
One dazzling rush,
Like a wild wish
Or blaze of truth.

First fire of age,
And the soft snow
Of ash below—
For the clean wood
The end was good;
For me, an image.

For then I saw
That fires, not I,
Burn down and die;
That flare of gold
Turns old, turns cold.
Not I. I grow.

Nor old, nor young,
The burning sprite
Of my delight,
A salamander
In fires of wonder,
Gives tongue, gives tongue!

MAY SARTON

REQUEST TO A YEAR

If the year is meditating a suitable gift,
I should like it to be the attitude
of my great-great-grandmother,
legendary devotee of the arts,

who, having had eight children
and little opportunity for painting pictures,
sat one day on a high rock
beside a river in Switzerland

and from a difficult distance viewed
her second son, balanced on a small ice-floe,
drift down the current towards a waterfall
that struck rock-bottom eighty feet below,

while her second daughter, impeded,
no doubt, by the petticoats of the day,
stretched out a last-hope alpenstock
(which luckily later caught him on his way).

Nothing, it was evident, could be done;
and with the artist's isolating eye
my great-great-grandmother hastily sketched the scene.
The sketch survives to prove the story by.

Year, if you have no Mother's day present planned;
reach back and bring me the firmness of her hand.

JUDITH WRIGHT

WOMEN LAUGHING

Gurgles, genderless,
Inside the incurious womb.

Random soliloquies of babies
Tickled by everything.

Undomesticated shrieks
Of small girls. Mother prophesies
You'll be crying in a minute.

Adolescents wearing giggles
Like chain-mail, against embarrassment,
Giggles formal in shape as
Butterpats, or dropped stitches.

Young women anxious to please,
Laughing eagerly before the punchline
(Being too naïve to know which it is).

Wives gleaming sleekly in public at
Husbandly jokes, masking
All trace of old acquaintance.

Mums obliging with rhetorical
Guffaws at the children's riddles
That bored their parents.

Old women, unmanned, free
Of children, embarrassment, desire to please,
Hooting grossly, without explanation.

U. A. FANTHORPE

THE CRAZY WOMAN

I shall not sing a May song.
A May song should be gay.
I'll wait until November
And sing a song of gray.

I'll wait until November.
That is the time for me.
I'll go out in the frosty dark
And sing most terribly.

And all the little people
Will stare at me and say,
"That is the Crazy Woman
Who would not sing in May."

GWENDOLYN BROOKS

NIGHT GIVES OLD WOMAN THE WORD

Dark whispers
behind the echo
of the wind. Mind
is trapped by patterns
in the sound.
Night works a spell—
Moon spills her naked light.
Reflected fire illuminates
the ground. The pull
of night words makes Earth-Woman
give off heat. Soil glistens
dampened by her sweat.
Corn seed feels the planet's turn,
unrolls her root,
prepares to send a shoot
above the dirt. Moon
attracting water in the veins
makes corn leaves uncurl
and probe nocturnal air.
The leaves stretch out
to catch the coming dew.
Clan mother, watching,
hears the planets move.
Old, clan mother listens
to the words—all nature
speaks as slowly seasons
turn—marked by the waxing,
waning Moon; messages
become imprinted on old bones.
Earth works in dark
as well as light. Life
moves in constant spiral
through the sky. We plant;
we harvest, and, at last,
we feast. Clan mother listens
and is filled with thanks.
Night murmurs and plants
grow in the fields.
Old Woman hears dark
speak the ancient word.

GAIL TREMBLAY

RIDE THE TURTLE'S BACK

A woman grows hard and skinny.
She squeezes into small corners.
Her quick eyes uncover dust and cobwebs.
She reaches out
for flint and sparks fly in the air.
Flames turned loose on fields
burn down to bare seeds
we planted deep.

The corn is white and sweet.
Under its pale, perfect kernels
a rotting cob is betrayal.
It lies in our bloated stomachs.

I lie in Grandmother's bed
and dream the earth into a turtle.
She carries us slowly across the universe.
The sun warms us.
At night the stars do tricks.
The moon caresses us.

We are listening for the sounds of food.
Mother is giving birth, Grandmother says.
Corn whispers.
The earth groans with labor
turning corn yellow in the sun.

I lie in Grandmother's bed.

We listen.

BETH BRANT

INDEX OF POETS

INDEX OF TITLES AND FIRST LINES

Titles are in *italics*. When the title and the first line are the same, the first line only is listed.

ACKNOWLEDGMENTS

Anna Akhmatova: "I taught myself to live simply and wisely" translated by Richard McKane from *Akhmatova: Selected Poems*, translation copyright © Richard McKane 1966 (Penguin Modern European Poets, 1969).

Margarita Aliger: "I Live with a Bullet" translated by Daniel Weissbort, from *20th Century Russian Poetry* by Yevgeny Yevtushenko, copyright © 1993 by Doubleday, a division of Bantam Doubleday Dell Publishing Group, Inc., reprinted by permission of Doubleday, a division of Random House, Inc.

Hira Bansode: "Woman" translated by Vinay Dharwadker, from *The Oxford Anthology of Modern Indian Poetry* edited by V. Dharwadker and A. K. Ramanujan (OUP, 1994), reprinted by permission of Oxford University Press, New Delhi.

Eavan Boland: "It's a Woman's World" copyright © 1982 by Eavan Boland, from *An Origin Like Water: Collected Poems 1967-1987* and from *Collected Poems* (Carcanet, 1989), reprinted by permission of W. W. Norton & Company, Inc., and of Carcanet Press Ltd.

Beth Brant: "Ride the Turtle's Back" from *A Mohawk Trail* by Beth Brant (Firebrand Books, Ithaca, New York, 1985), copyright © 1985 by Beth Brant, reprinted by permission of the publishers.

Gwendolyn Brooks: "Mrs. Small" and "The Crazy Woman" from *Blacks* (Third World Press, Chicago, 1991), copyright © Gwendolyn Brooks 1991, reprinted by permission of the author.

Ch'iu Chin: "To the Tune 'The River Is Red'" from *Women Poets of China* translated and edited by Kenneth Rexroth and Ling Chung, copyright © 1973 by Kenneth Rexroth and Ling Chung, reprinted by permission of New Directions Publishing Corp.

Sandra Cisneros: "My Wicked Wicked Ways" from *My Wicked Wicked Ways*, copyright © 1987 by Sandra Cisneros (Third Woman Press, 1987, Alfred A. Knopf,1989), reprinted by permission of Susan Bergholz Literary Services, New York. All rights reserved.

Lucille Clifton: "My Mama Moved Among the Days" from *Good Woman: Poems and a Memoir 1969-1980*, copyright © 1987 by Lucille Clifton, reprinted by permission of the publisher, BOA Editions, Ltd.

Wendy Cope: "Sisters" from *Is That the New Moon?* (Lions, Teen Tracks, 1989), reprinted by permission of the Peters Fraser & Dunlop Group Ltd.

Rosemary Dobson: "Folding the Sheets" from *Collected Poems* (Angus & Robertson, 1991), reprinted by permission of the copyright holder, c/o Curtis Brown (Aust) Pty Ltd.

Carol Ann Duffy: "The Good Teachers" from *Mean Time* (Anvil Press Poetry, 1993), reprinted by permission of the publisher.

Mari Evans: ". . . And the Old Women Gathered" from *I Am a Black Woman* (Wm. Morrow, 1970).

U. A. Fanthorpe: "Women Laughing" from *Voices Off* (Peterloo Poets, 1984), © U. A. Fanthorpe, reprinted by permission of the publisher.

Jane Flanders: "Twirling" from *Timepiece*, copyright © 1988 by Jane Flanders, reprinted by permission of the publisher, the University of Pittsburgh Press.

Karen Gershon: "To My Children" from *Collected Poems* (Papermac, an imprint of Macmillan, 1990), reprinted by permission of the publisher.

Nigâr Hanim: "Tell Me Again" translated by Tâlat S. Halman from *The Penguin Book of Women Poets* edited by Carol Cosman et al (Allen Lane, 1978), reprinted by permission of Tâlat S. Halman.

Linda Hogan: "The Truth Is" from *Seeing Through the Sun* (University of Massachusetts Press, 1985), copyright © 1985 by the University of Massachusetts Press, reprinted by permission of the publisher.

Rashidah Ismaili: "Yet Still" from *Oniybo and Other Poems* (Shamal Books Inc., 1985).

Elizabeth Jennings: "The Second World War" from *Collected Poems* (Macmillan), reprinted by permission of David Higham Associates.

Mamta Kalia: "After Eight Years of Marriage" from *Nine Indian Women Poets: An Anthology* edited by Eunice de Souza (Oxford University Press India, 1997), reprinted by permission of the author.

Marie Luise Kaschnitz: "Return to Frankfurt" from *Überallenie, Ausgewählte Gedichte 1928-1965* (Classen Verlag, 1965), in translation by Beatrice Cameron, reprinted by permission of Verlagshaus Goethestrasse GmbH & Co, KG.

Antigone Kefala: "Freedom Fighter" from *Absence: New and Selected Poems* (Hale & Iremonger, 1998), reprinted by permission of the publisher.

Nagase Kiyoko: "Surf" translated by Kijima Hajime from *A Zigzag Joy: A Bilingual Anthology of Contemporary Japanese Poetry* (Doyo Bijutsusha Shuppan Hanbai), copyright © Kijima Hajime 1998, reprinted by permission of the translator and editor, Kijima Hajime.

Dorothy Livesay: "Eve" from *Collected Poems: The Two Seasons* (McGraw Hill Ryerson, 1972), reprinted by permission of the Estate of Dorothy Livesay.

Liz Lochhead: "Poem for My Sister" from *Dreaming Frankenstein and Collected Poems* (Polygon Books, 1984), reprinted by permission of Edinburgh University Press Ltd.

Marjorie Oludhe Macgoye: "A Freedom Song" from *Song of Nyarloka and Other Poems* (OUP, 1977), reprinted by permission of Oxford University Press, Eastern Africa.

Nāzik al-Malā'ikah: "Elegy for a Woman of No Importance" translated by Chris Knipp and Mohammad Sadiq from *The Other Voice: Twentieth Century Women's Verse in Translation* edited by Joanna Bankier et al (W. W. Norton, 1976) originally from *Qurārat al-Mawja*, copyright © 1957 by Nāzik al-Malā'ikah (Dar al Awda, Beirut).

Ileana Mălăncioiu: "My Sister, the Empress" translated by Dan Duțescu from *An Anthology of Romanian Women Poets* edited by Adam J. Sorkin & Kurt W. Treptow (East European Monographs in association with the Romanian Cultural Foundation Publishing House, distributed by Columbia University Press, 1994), copyright © 1994 by East European Monographs, reprinted by permission of East European Monographs.

Harryette Mullen: "Momma Sayings" from *Tree Tall Woman* (Energy Earth Communications, Galveston, Texas, 1981), copyright © 1981 by Haryette Mullen.

Kim Nam-jo: "My Baby Has No Name Yet" translated by Ko Won from *Contemporary Korean Poetry* (University of Iowa Press).

Grace Nichols: "Holding My Beads" from *I Is a Long Memoried Woman* (Karnak House, 1983), copyright © Grace Nichols 1983, reprinted by permission of Curtis Brown Ltd, London, on behalf of the author.

Ibaragi Noriko: "When I Was at My Most Beautiful" translated by L. Lowitz and M. Aoyama from *Other Side River: Free Verse*, Contemporary Japanese Women's Poetry, volume 2, edited and translated by Leza Lowitz and Miyuki Aoyama (Stone Bridge Press, 1995), reprinted by permission of the publisher.

Dorothy Parker: "Chant for Dark Hours" from *The Portable Dorothy Parker* (Viking Penguin), copyright 1928, renewed © 1956 by Dorothy Parker, and from *The Collected Poems of Dorothy Parker* (Duckworth), reprinted by permission of the publishers, Viking Penguin, a division of Penguin Putnam, Inc., and Duckworth and Co. Ltd.

Linda Pastan: "To a Daughter Leaving Home" from *Carnival Evening: New and Selected Poems* 1968-1998, copyright © 1998 by Linda Pastan, reprinted by permission of the publisher, W. W. Norton & Company, Inc.

Eva Picková: "Fear" from *I Never Saw Another Butterfly: Children's Drawings and Poems from Terezín Concentration Camp 1942-1944*, edited by Hana Volaková (McGraw-Hill 1962).

Sylvia Plath: "Morning Song" from *Ariel*, copyright © 1961 by Ted Hughes, also from *Collected Poems* (Faber), reprinted by permission of the publishers HarperCollins Publishers, Inc., and Faber & Faber Ltd.

Adrienne Rich: "Upper Broadway" from *The Fact of a Doorframe: Poems Selected and New 1950-1984*, copyright © 1984 by Adrienne Rich, copyright © 1975, 1978 by W. W. Norton & Company, Inc., copyright © 1981 by Adrienne Rich, reprinted by permission of the author and the publisher, W. W. Norton & Company, Inc.

Elizabeth Riddell: "News of a Baby" from *Selected Poems* (ETT Imprint, Sydney, 1992), reprinted by permission of the publisher.

Judith Rodriguez: "Eskimo Occasion" from *New and Collected Poems* (University of Queensland Press, 1988), reprinted by permission of the publisher.

Kurihara Sadako: "Let Us Be Midwives!" from *Black Eggs* by Kurihara Sadako, translated by Richard H. Minear, Michigan Monographs Series in Japanese Studies, No 12 (Center for Japanese Studies, The University of Michigan, Ann Arbor, 1994), reprinted by permission of the publisher.

Sonia Sanchez: "Earth Mother" from *I've Been a Woman: New and Selected Poems* (Third World Press, 1985), copyright © 1985 by Sonia Sanchez, reprinted by permission of the author.

May Sarton: "On a Winter Night" from *Collected Poems 1930-1993*, copyright © 1993, 1988, 1984, 1980, 1974 by May Sarton, reprinted by permission of the publisher, W. W. Norton & Company, Inc., and from *Coming Into Eighty* (The Women's Press, 1995), by permission of the publisher.

Stevie Smith: "Dear Female Heart" from *The Collected Poems of Stevie Smith* (Penguin 20th Century Classics/New Directions), copyright © 1972 by Stevie Smith, reprinted by permission of James MacGibbon and New Directions Publishing Corp.

Edith Södergran: "Vierge Moderne" translated by Stina Katchadourian, from *Selected Poems 1916-1923* (Fjord, 1981).

Gertrude Stein: "What Do I See" and "Why Do You Feel Differently" from "A Valentine to Sherwood Anderson" in *Writings 1903-1932* (The Library of America), reprinted by permission of David Higham Associates.

PICTURE CREDITS